RICKY RICOTTA'S
MIGHTY ROBOT

vs. THE UNPLEASANT PENGUINS FROM PLUTO

STORY BY
DAV PILKEY

ART BY
DAN SANTAT

SCHOLASTIC INC.

FOR AMELIA AND EDISON ELTING
– D.P.

FOR DAV AND SAYURI: THANKS FOR
LETTING ME TAKE PART IN THIS JOURNEY.
– D.S.

Text copyright © 2016 by Dav Pilkey
www.pilkey.com

Illustrations copyright © 2016 by Dan Santat
www.dantat.com

Library of Congress Cataloging-in-Publication Data

Pilkey, Dav, 1966 – author.
Ricky Ricotta's mighty robot vs. the unpleasant penguins from Pluto /
story by Dav Pilkey ; art by Dan Santat.
pages cm
Summary: Infuriated by the declaration that Pluto is no longer a planet, President Penguin
and his penguins invade Earth and it is up to Ricky and his robot pal to defeat them — with
some help from Ricky's cousin Lucy and her pets.
1. Ricotta, Ricky (Fictitious character) — Juvenile fiction. 2. Mice — Juvenile fiction.
3. Robots — Juvenile fiction. 4. Heroes — Juvenile fiction. 5. Penguins — Juvenile fiction.
6. Cousins — Juvenile fiction. 7. Pluto (Dwarf planet) — Juvenile fiction. [1. Mice — Fiction.
2. Robots — Fiction. 3. Heroes — Fiction. 4. Penguins — Fiction. 5. Cousins — Fiction.
6. Pluto (Dwarf planet) — Fiction.] I. Santat, Dan, illustrator. II. Title. III.
Title: Ricky Ricotta's mighty robot versus the unpleasant penguins from Pluto.
PZ7.P63123Rtn 2016   813.54 — dc23   2015002256

ISBN 978-0-545-63017-7

10 9 8 7 6 5 4 3 2   16 17 18 19 20

Printed in the U.S.A. 40

First printing: June 2016

Book design by Phil Falco

CHAPTERS

CHAPTER ONE
THE POND

Ricky Ricotta and his Mighty Robot were having a relaxing day floating in their new pond.

"This is the life," said Ricky. "Nothing but peace and quiet and—"

"And *LUCY!*" cried Ricky's cousin,
Lucy, as she bounded from her parents'
car. Lucy's three pets, Fudgie,
Cupcake, and Waffles, raced after her.
Boing! Boing! Boing! Boing! Boing!

Lucy and her pets made quite
a splash.

Fudgie and Cupcake each did a
belly flop off the roof of the house.

Waffles started a water fight
with his wings.

And Lucy laughed and screamed
and ran around like a maniac.
"This is FUN!" cried Lucy.
"This *WAS* fun," said Ricky.

CHAPTER TWO

RUINED

Ricky and his Mighty Robot couldn't
take it anymore. They got out of
the pond and sat on the front
steps, sulking.

"Hey, Ricky," cried Lucy.
"Aren't ya coming back in the
pond? I poured in a bunch
of pink bubble bath! Now
it's *glamorous!*"

When Ricky and his Mighty
Robot saw the pond, they were
very upset.

"NOOOO!" cried Ricky. "You
RUINED it!"

Ricky marched into the backyard where the adults were playing cards.

"MOMMMM!" cried Ricky. "Lucy made our pond all pink and bubbly!"

"Why, that sounds like fun," said Ricky's mom.

"It's *NOT* fun! It's *STUPID*!" Ricky shouted. "Every time we start to have fun around here, Lucy has to come along and *RUIN* it!"

"*RICKY RICOTTA*," exclaimed Ricky's father. "You have a BAD attitude. You need to apologize *RIGHT NOW!*"

But before Ricky could get the chance, Lucy started to cry.

"I'm sorry, Ricky," Lucy sobbed. "I just wanted to play with you! I didn't mean to ruin everything."

"I think we'd better go now," said Uncle Freddie.

Ricky's aunt and uncle helped everybody get into the car, and soon they were all on their way back home.

Ricky felt terrible.
Ricky's Mighty Robot felt
terrible, too.

CHAPTER THREE
PRESIDENT PENGUIN

Meanwhile, 4.6 billion miles away
on the frozen surface of Pluto,
someone else was feeling terrible,
too. His name was President Penguin,
and he was the leader of Pluto.

I'M THE BOSS

President Penguin had just finished
drinking his cup of ice cubes and
had settled in to read his morning
newspaper. Then he saw the headline:
PLUTO NO LONGER A PLANET

"What's THIS?!!?" cried President Penguin.

"I think it's a newspaper," said his guard Clancy.

"Yep," said his other guard Nigel. "That's a newspaper, all right."

"OF COURSE IT'S A NEWSPAPER, YOU NINCOMPOOPS!" President Penguin screamed. "I'm talking about this *HEADLINE*!"

President Penguin read the story out loud. "'Scientists from Squeakyville declare that Pluto is not a planet after all. It is too small and too far away from the sun. Pluto has been renamed a *gassy ice dwarf.*'"

"I guess you're no longer the president of *Planet* Pluto," said Clancy. "Now you're the president of *Gassy Ice Dwarf* Pluto."

"That doesn't have quite the same ring to it," said Nigel.

"SILENCE, YOU FOOLS!" cried President Penguin. "Those Earthlings can't disrespect us like that! Get my spaceship ready. We're going to Squeakyville to teach them some manners!"

"Yes, Sir!" squawked Nigel and Clancy.

CHAPTER FOUR
OFF TO EARTH WE GO

President Penguin's army quickly prepared his spaceship for takeoff. The captain tested the controls, the first mate checked the mirrors, and Nigel and Clancy put on their space suits.

"Hey!" cried President Penguin. "Where is *MY* space suit? I can't attack Earth in my pajamas!"

"Of course you can't," said Clancy. "Earth would never fit in your pajamas!"

"I agree," said Nigel. "Your pajamas are much too small."

"*SILENCE, YOU FOOLS!*" cried President Penguin. He grabbed a space suit from the dirty-laundry basket, stuffed himself in it, and waddled into the cargo bay.

Soon they were all aboard and ready to go. The turbo boosters fired up, and the spaceship lifted off toward Earth.

"How soon until we get to Squeakyville?" asked President Penguin.

"We should arrive tomorrow morning," said the captain.

"Excellent!" said President Penguin. "Earth will regret the day it ever dishonored Planet Pluto!"

CHAPTER FIVE
MAKING AMENDS

That night, Ricky and his Robot were having a hard time getting to sleep.

"I feel so bad about being mean to Lucy today," said Ricky. "I wish I could make amends to her somehow."

Ricky's Robot did not understand.

"Making amends is something you *do* to show someone how sorry you are," said Ricky. "It is easy to *SAY* you're sorry. But if you're REALLY sorry, you must *DO* something about it."

Ricky's Robot got an idea. He pointed to the flower bed.

"Oh, yeah!" said Ricky. "Lucy *loves* flowers. Let's plant a bunch of flowers for her!"

So Ricky and his Mighty Robot flew off to find some flowers for Lucy.

Quickly, they flew to Hawaii, where it was still light outside. They saw lots and lots of beautiful wildflowers growing on the side of a volcano.

"Let's use these!" said Ricky.

So the Mighty Robot scooped up as many flowers as he could carry, and they flew back home.

When they returned, they decided to plant the flowers on the side of the tallest mountain in Squeakyville. Ricky and his Robot planted flowers all night long.

When the sun rose the next morning, they were finished.

HOORAY FOR LUCY

Ricky and his Mighty Robot were very tired.

"Let's go home and get some shut-eye," said Ricky. So they flew back to their house and got ready for bed.

CHAPTER SIX
THE ARRIVAL

At that very moment, President Penguin's spaceship was entering Earth's atmosphere.

"We'll be in Squeakyville soon, Sir," said the captain.

"Wonderful!" said President Penguin. "Let's land down there on that mountain so everybody can see us!"

"OK," said the captain. He reversed the rocket thrusters and landed their spaceship gently and quietly on top of the mountain.

FOR
LUCY

CHAPTER SEVEN
GUARD THE SHIP

President Penguin led his captain and first mate downstairs to the cargo bay. Then they each climbed aboard a giant, armored Penguin-Mobile.

"Listen up!" cried President Penguin. "Today, we fight for HONOR! We fight for RESPECT! We fight for—"

"Can we help?" Nigel interrupted.

"Yeah!" said Clancy. "We could pass out refreshments to the Earthlings!"

"You don't pass out *refreshments* at a battle," yelled President Penguin. "Just stay here and guard the ship!"

"OK," said Nigel. "You can count on us!"

The cargo-bay door opened, and the three Penguin-Mobiles rolled out to begin their savage and ruthless attack.

"Hey, look," said Lucy. "Some penguin robots are coming out of our castle! Awww, how cute!"

Soon Lucy and Waffles reached the cargo-bay door. Fudgie and Cupcake ran up behind them, huffing and puffing.

"Halt!" cried Clancy and Nigel. "Who goes there?"

"Step aside, dudes," said Lucy. "We're here to check out my new castle!"

"Oh, this isn't a castle," said Nigel proudly. "It's a spaceship."

"It is *too* a castle," said Lucy. "My cousin, Ricky, built it for me! Don't you guys know *anything*?"

The two guards were very confused.

"Ummm . . ." said Clancy. "We're not supposed to—"

"Listen," Lucy interrupted. "*I'M* the princess! This is *MY* castle! And you guys have to do what *I* say! Any questions?"

"Are you *really* a princess?" asked Nigel.

"Of course I am!" cried Lucy. "It says so right here on my dress! Now get outta my way before I throw you guys in the dungeon!"

"Yes, Ma'am," said the two guards.

Lucy, Fudgie, Cupcake, and Waffles climbed into the cargo bay and looked around.

"WOW, this is *SO COOL!*" said Lucy. "Hey, do you guys have anything to eat around here?"

"Of course, Your Majesty," said Clancy. "Right this way!"

The two guards led Lucy and her pets to the kitchen.

"We've got all kinds of food," said Nigel. "We've got hamburgers, hot dogs, potato chips, pizza, grilled-cheese sandwiches, French fries, chocolate cake, coconut-cream pie, cotton candy, doughnuts, vanilla soda, popcorn, gummy spiders, banana splits, jelly beans, bubble gum, chocolate-chip cookies . . . and vegetables!"

"That sounds yummy," said Lucy.
"Bring it on, bub!"

"Hooray!" cried Nigel and Clancy. They took off their helmets, put on their chef hats, and began preparing a gigantic feast.

CHAPTER EIGHT
THE ATTACK BEGINS

Ricky and his Mighty Robot were
sound asleep. Suddenly, they heard
a terrible crash.

"What was THAT?!!?" cried Ricky.

Ricky's Robot peered out the window with his telescopic eyeball. He saw three Penguin-Mobiles attacking Squeakyville.

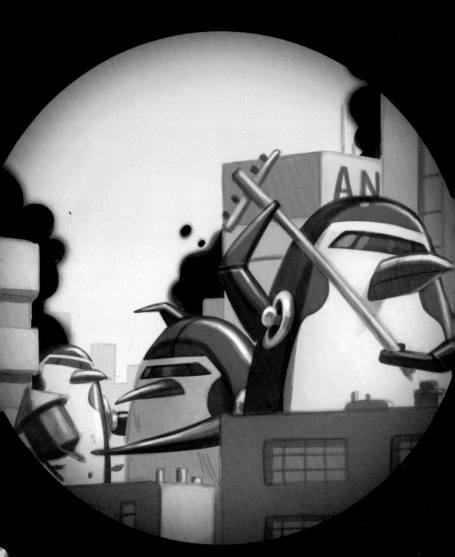

"Well, buddy," said Ricky. "It looks like we've got a city to save!"

Quickly, they made their way to the center of town.

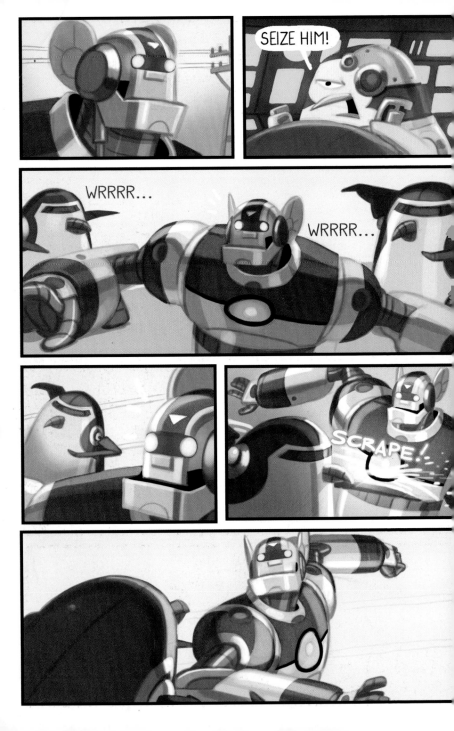

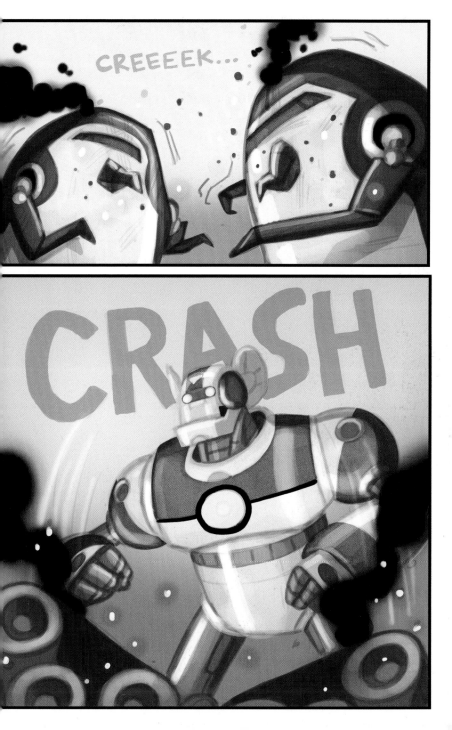

CRUNCH

SLAM

CRASH

CHAPTER NINE
THE BIG BATTLE
(IN FLIP-O-RAMA™)

FLIP-O
HEY, KIDS! YOU CAN ANIMATE THE ACTION BY FOLLOWING THESE EASY STEPS!

-RAMA
HERE'S HOW IT WORKS!

STEP 1
Place your *left* hand inside the dotted lines marked "LEFT HAND HERE." Hold the book open *flat*.

STEP 2
Grasp the *right-hand* page with your right thumb and index finger (inside the dotted lines marked "RIGHT THUMB HERE").

STEP 3
Now *quickly* flip the right-hand page back and forth until the picture appears to be *animated*.

(For extra fun, try adding your own sound-effects!)

FLIP-O-RAMA 1

(pages 69 and 71)

Remember, flip *only* page 69.
While you are flipping, be sure you
can see the picture on page 69
and the one on page 71.
If you flip quickly, the two
pictures will start to look like
<u>one</u> *animated* picture.

Don't forget to add
your own sound-effects!

LEFT HAND HERE

THE PENGUIN-MOBILE ATTACKED.

RIGHT
THUMB
HERE

RIGHT
INDEX
FINGER
HERE

70

THE PENGUIN-MOBILE ATTACKED.

FLIP-O-RAMA 2

(pages 73 and 75)

Remember, flip *only* page 73.
While you are flipping, be sure you
can see the picture on page 73
and the one on page 75.
If you flip quickly, the two
pictures will start to look like
<u>one</u> *animated* picture.

Don't forget to add
your own sound-effects!

LEFT HAND HERE

RICKY'S ROBOT
FOUGHT BACK.

RIGHT
THUMB
HERE

RICKY'S ROBOT
FOUGHT BACK.

FLIP-O-RAMA 3

(pages 77 and 79)

Remember, flip *only* page 77.
While you are flipping, be sure you
can see the picture on page 77
and the one on page 79.
If you flip quickly, the two
pictures will start to look like
<u>one</u> *animated* picture.

Don't forget to add
your own sound-effects!

LEFT HAND HERE

RICKY'S ROBOT BATTLED HARD.

RIGHT
THUMB
HERE

78

RICKY'S ROBOT
BATTLED HARD.

FLIP-O-RAMA 4

(pages 81 and 83)

Remember, flip *only* page 81.
While you are flipping, be sure you
can see the picture on page 81
and the one on page 83.
If you flip quickly, the two
pictures will start to look like
one *animated* picture.

Don't forget to add
your own sound-effects!

LEFT HAND HERE

THE PENGUIN-MOBILES
BATTLED HARDER.

RIGHT
THUMB
HERE

THE PENGUIN-MOBILES
BATTLED HARDER.

FLIP-O-RAMA 5

(pages 85 and 87)

Remember, flip *only* page 85.
While you are flipping, be sure you
can see the picture on page 85
and the one on page 87.
If you flip quickly, the two
pictures will start to look like
<u>one</u> *animated* picture.

Don't forget to add
your own sound-effects!

LEFT HAND HERE

RICKY'S ROBOT
LOST THE WAR.

RIGHT
THUMB
HERE

RICKY'S ROBOT LOST THE WAR.

The big battle had caused quite a loud ruckus. The terrible noise reached all the way up to the mountaintop.

"What is going on out there?" cried Lucy. "It's so noisy, I can't even hear myself ea*t*!"

Fudgie and Cupcake looked
out the window. They saw Ricky's
Mighty Robot buried in the
ice. They saw the victorious
Penguin-Mobiles celebrating.

Fudgie and Cupcake panicked.
They jumped and whined and ran
around in circles.

"What's the matter with them?"
asked Clancy.

"Oh, they're just hyper," said
Lucy. "They get that way when they
eat too much candy."

But Fudgie and Cupcake would
not settle down. They pointed and
roared and scratched on the window.

"WOULD YOU GUYS *CHILL?*"
shouted Lucy. "I *TOLD* you not to eat
all those gummy spiders!"

Finally, Cupcake could take it no longer. He ran and grabbed Lucy in his mouth and carried her to the window. Lucy looked out.

"HEY!" cried Lucy. "That's the Mighty Robot! He got *FROZED*!"

Nigel, Clancy, Fudgie, and Waffles rushed to the window and looked out, too.

"What are those penguin robots doing?" asked Lucy.

"Oh, those are *our* guys," said Clancy proudly. "We're invading Earth!"

"You're *WHAT*?!!?" cried Lucy.
"What's *WRONG* WITH YOU?!!?"

"It—it wasn't *our* idea," cried Nigel.
"Our president was mad because *your*
scientists said Pluto wasn't a planet
anymore."

"Who *cares*?" said Lucy. "You can't
start a fight just because you don't
like what somebody says. Even I know
that, and I'm only *five*!"

"I'm sorry, Your Highness," said Nigel.

"I'm sorry, too," Clancy cried.

"If you're REALLY sorry," said Lucy, "don't just SAY it! You'd better *DO* something about it!"

Lucy stuffed some jelly beans into her pocket and ran down the stairs to the cargo bay. "C'mon, Fudgie and Cupcake and Waffles!" Lucy yelled. "We gotta go!"

"Where are you going?" cried Clancy.
"We've gotta save Ricky and his Robot,"
Lucy shouted. "They're our *cousins!*"

CHAPTER ELEVEN

LUCY TO THE RESCUE

Lucy jumped onto Waffles's back, and together they shot off toward the city. Fudgie and Cupcake followed behind them, tearing through the terrain as fast as they could run.

Meanwhile, down in the city, things were getting much worse for Ricky and his Robot. President Penguin found Ricky on the rooftop and scooped him up in his giant metallic flipper.

"So, you thought you could defeat us with your wimpy Robot, did you?" snarled President Penguin.

"We're *still* gonna win," said Ricky, as he struggled to get free. "We *always* win!"

"Oh, *REALLY*?" President Penguin laughed. "You're doing a *great* job! Bravo!"

Just then, Lucy and Waffles
soared in through the clouds.
"YOU LET GO OF MY COUSIN,
YA BIG BULLY!" cried Lucy.

"WHAT?" cried President Penguin. "HOW *DARE* YOU?!!?"

Lucy reached into her pocket and pulled out a handful of jelly beans. She threw them at President Penguin with all her might.

"Hey! STOP THAT!" cried President Penguin. "OW! Those really *hurt!*"

He reached out with his other metallic flipper, grabbed Lucy and Waffles, and held them tightly.

Suddenly, Fudgie and Cupcake came bounding over, roaring ferociously. They grabbed President Penguin's tank treads with their teeth and shook their heads back and forth. They would not let go.

"HAW! HAW! HAW!" laughed
President Penguin. He looked
Ricky in the eye. "Is *THIS* how
you're going to win? SERIOUSLY?
Is *that* all you've got?"

CHAPTER TWELVE
RIGHT GUARDS

Suddenly, a whistling sound came from the mountain.

"What's that noise?" cried President Penguin.

It was the sound of two missiles. They screamed down from the spaceship and slammed directly into the two Penguin-Mobiles guarding Ricky's Robot.

Ka-POW! Ka-POW!

Both Penguin-Mobiles burst into flames.

"I've been hit!" cried the captain. He jumped out of his cockpit and flew away.

"Me, too," cried the first mate. He tumbled out of his Penguin-Mobile and fluttered off.

"Wait a minute," said Ricky. "Penguins can't fly!"

"Oh, yeah," said the captain and the first mate, and they fell to the ground, screaming.

"Wh-What's going on?" cried President Penguin.

"It's just us," yelled Nigel and Clancy from the spaceship. "We're making amends!"

Suddenly, another whistling sound came from the spaceship. It was a third missile, and it was headed directly at President Penguin.

FIRE
MISSILE

KA-POW!

The Penguin-Mobile exploded. Ricky and Lucy and Waffles fell from the giant metal flippers. Lucy grabbed on to Waffles's neck.

"C'mon, Waffles!" cried Lucy. "We gotta catch Ricky. He's falling!"

Waffles flapped his wings and swooped down after Ricky. But he was not quick enough. Ricky fell faster and faster toward the ground below.

CHAPTER THIRTEEN
RICKY'S MIGHTY ROBOT THAWS OUT

Suddenly, a giant metal hand shot out and caught Ricky. It was the Mighty Robot.

The heat from the burning Penguin-Mobiles had thawed him out just in time.

The Mighty Robot pulled himself
from the wet, crackling ice and grabbed
President Penguin.

"I *TOLD* you we'd win," said Ricky.

CHAPTER FOURTEEN
BACK TO PLUTO

Ricky and his Mighty Robot took
President Penguin to the Squeakyville
jail where he belonged . . .

UNDER CONSTRUCTION
WE'RE EXPANDING!

. . . while Lucy and her pets marched the captain and the first mate back to the spaceship.

"You guys better get out of here before Ricky and his Robot get back," said Lucy.

"But what about our president?" asked Nigel.

"Yeah," said Clancy. "Pluto *needs* a president!"

"Ya don't need that bully," said Lucy. "I hereby declare that YOU two guys are the new presidents . . . of *PLANET* Pluto!"

"*PLANET* Pluto?" cried Nigel. "D-Do you really mean it?"

"Sure I do," said Lucy. "After all, I'm a princess. What I say goes!"

"Oh, *THANK YOU*, Lucy!" cried President Nigel. "We'll miss you!"

"Good-bye, Lucy," sobbed President Clancy. "We'll never forget you!"

"Come back and see me sometime," said Lucy.

"We will," said the penguins, as they waddled back to their spaceship and blasted off for home.

CHAPTER FIFTEEN
PINK POND PARTY

The next day, Ricky and his Mighty Robot threw a pool party for Lucy and her pets.

They all laughed and splashed and had a wonderful time.

"I'm glad to see that you and Lucy are having fun together," said Ricky's mom.

"Yes," said Ricky's dad. "Thank you for apologizing and for making amends."

"No problem," said Ricky . . .

... "that's what friends are for!"

READY FOR

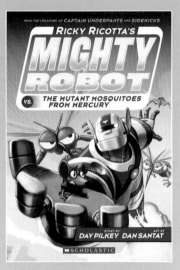

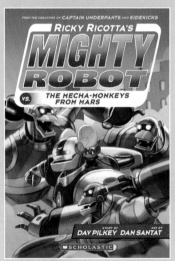

MORE RICKY?

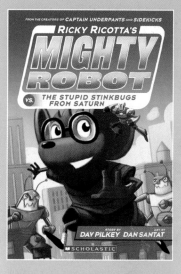

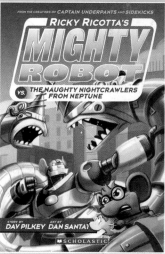

DAV PILKEY

has written and illustrated more than fifty books for children, including *The Paperboy*, a Caldecott Honor book; *Dog Breath: The Horrible Trouble with Hally Tosis*, winner of the California Young Reader Medal; and the IRA Children's Choice Dumb Bunnies series. He is also the creator of the *New York Times* best-selling Captain Underpants books. Dav lives in the Pacific Northwest with his wife. Find him online at www.pilkey.com.

DAN SANTAT

is the writer and illustrator of the *New York Times* bestselling picture book *The Adventures of Beekle: The Unimaginary Friend*, which was awarded the Caldecott Medal. He is also the creator of the graphic novel *Sidekicks* and has illustrated many acclaimed picture books, including *Because I'm Your Dad* by Ahmet Zappa and *Crankenstein* by Samantha Berger. Dan also created the Disney animated hit *The Replacements*. He lives in Southern California with his family. Find him online at www.dantat.com.